The Lion Who
Wanted to Love

Also by Giles Andreae
and illustrated by David Wojtowycz
Rumble in the Jungle
A noisy collection
of animal poems

First published in the United States 1998 by
Little Tiger Press
N16 W23390 Stoneridge Drive, Waukesha, WI 53188
Originally published in Great Britain 1997 by
Orchard Books, London
Text © 1997 Giles Andreae
Illustrations © 1997 David Wojtowycz
Library of Congress Cataloging-in-Publication Data
Andreae, Giles, 1966-
The lion who wanted to love / Giles Andreae ; David Wojtowycz.
p.   cm.
Summary : A young lion decides he would rather be friends with
the other jungle animals than try to eat them.
ISBN 1-888444-25-8 (hc)
[1. Lions—Fiction. 2. Jungle animals—Fiction. 3. Friendship—
Fiction. 4. Stories in rhyme.] I. Wojtowycz, David, ill. II. Title.
PZ8.3.A54865Li 1997 [E]—dc21 97-24542 CIP AC
Printed in Belgium
First American Edition
1 3 5 7 9 10 8 6 4 2

The Lion Who Wanted to Love

Giles Andreae

David Wojtowycz

Little Tiger Press

To Victoria
G.A.

For T.C. and T.D.
D.W.

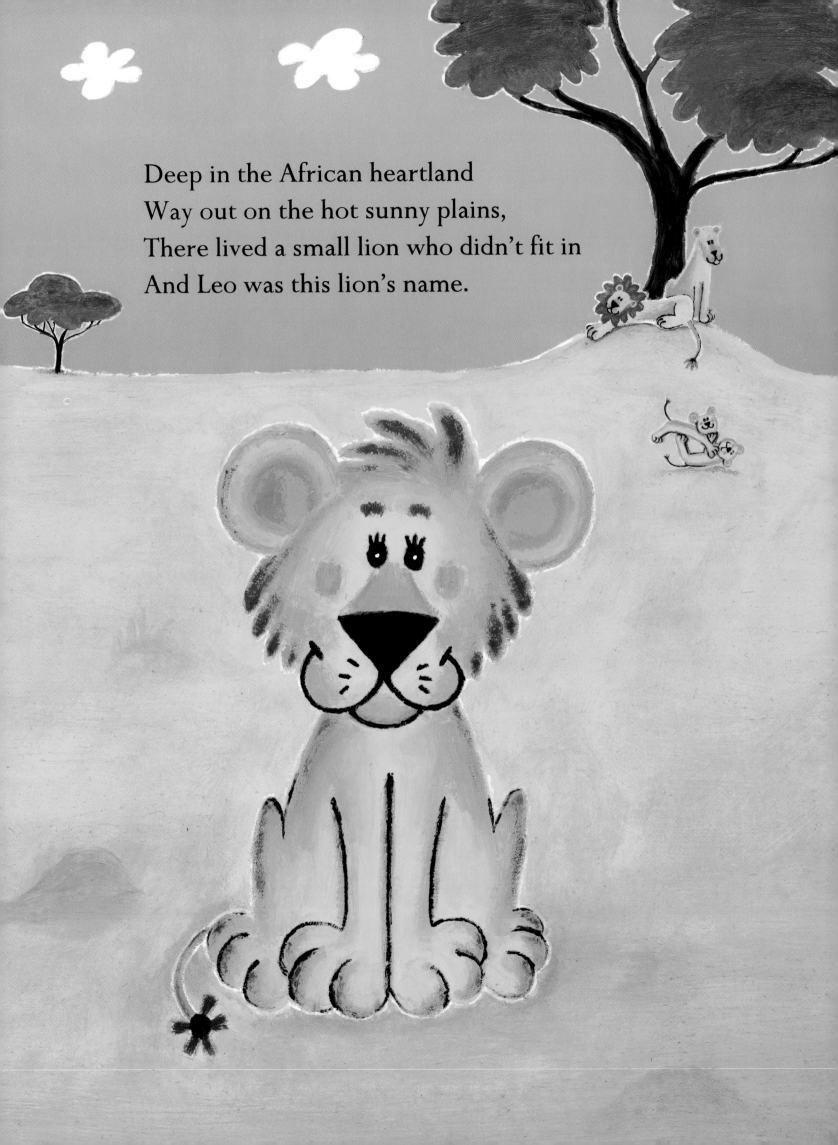

Deep in the African heartland
Way out on the hot sunny plains,
There lived a small lion who didn't fit in
And Leo was this lion's name.

Now lions are usually fierce
And lions are meant to be strong,
But Leo wanted to love everybody
And play with his friends all day long.

"You worry me, Leo, my darling,"
His mom started saying one day.
"You'll never survive in the animal world
If you don't learn to hunt for your prey."

"But, Mommy," said Leo, bewildered,
"I don't think I quite understand.
I know that most lions prefer to eat meat,
But I'd rather live off of the land."

"And besides, when I'm close to a zebra
A funny thought goes through my head,
Instead of deciding to bite through his skin
I'd much rather hug him instead."

"I have spoken," said Leo's mom sternly.
"It's up to you now to decide,
But if you insist that you're not going to hunt,
Then there's no place for you in our pride."

Poor Leo crept off to the jungle
But hoped that with love in his heart,
He'd learn how to cope in the animal world,
Though he didn't quite know where to start.

That evening while Leo was sleeping
He woke to the thunder of hooves,
And when he looked up from his lair he could see
A whole antelope herd on the move.

Some leopards were running beside them
Surrounded by thick clouds of dust.
Leo thought quickly and jumped to his feet,
"I must help them!" he cried. "Yes, I must!"

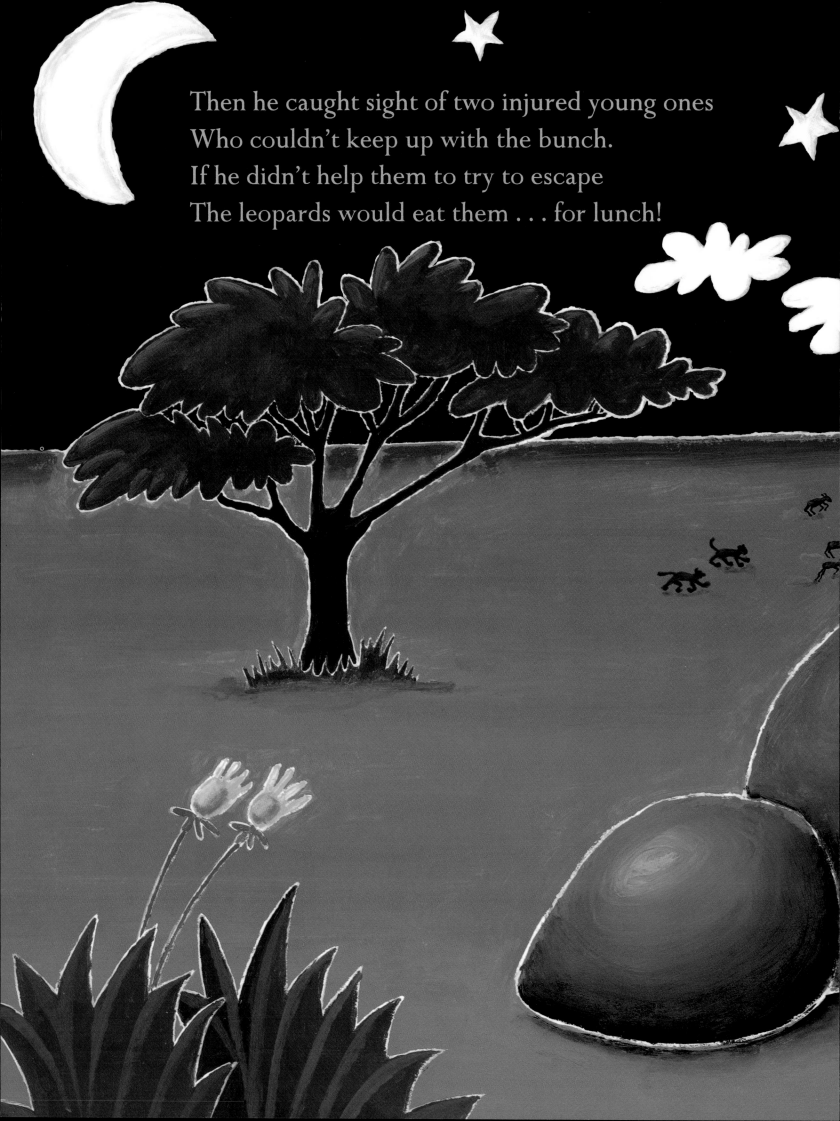

Then he caught sight of two injured young ones
Who couldn't keep up with the bunch.
If he didn't help them to try to escape
The leopards would eat them . . . for lunch!

Leo led them away to safety
And gave them some food they could eat.
He licked their wounds clean till they both became strong
And he nursed them back onto their feet.

The antelope babies kissed Leo
And told him, "We'll never forget
That you saved our lives when we thought we were dead,
You're the friendliest lion we've met."

Leo was awfully excited,
His face had lit up in a smile.
"It's fun making friends in the jungle," he thought.
Then he lay down and slept for a while.

From that day on Leo decided
To run to each squeal and each cry.
He led little hippos to watering holes
And he taught baby birds how to fly.

He helped a giraffe who'd been injured
And a vulture who'd hurt his wing.
And even though all of his friends gave him food,
He never once asked for a thing.

Then one day beside a wide river
Leo heard a small animal scream.
He ran to the bank and caught sight of a cheetah
Being swept very quickly downstream.

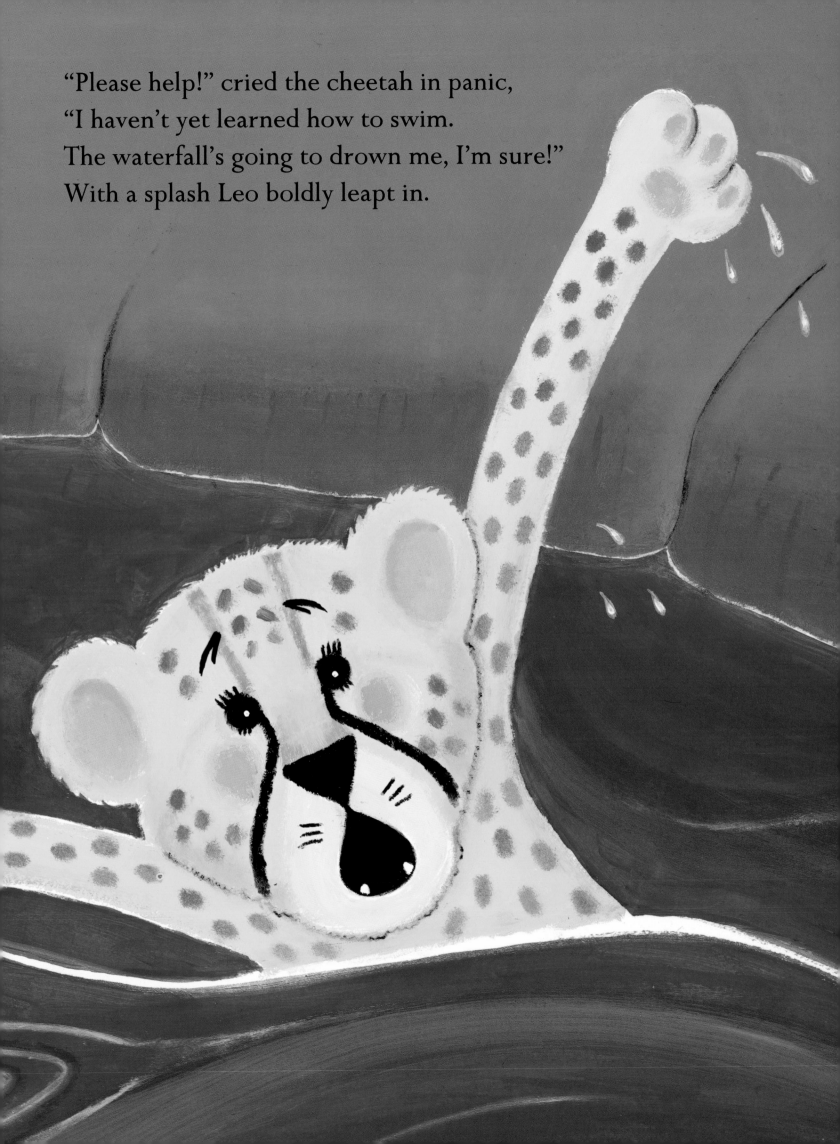

"Please help!" cried the cheetah in panic,
"I haven't yet learned how to swim.
The waterfall's going to drown me, I'm sure!"
With a splash Leo boldly leapt in.

He managed to rescue the cheetah
And push him quite safe to the side,
But as he was trying to scramble ashore
Leo slipped and got caught in the tide.

The river was crashing and foaming,
And Leo let out a loud yelp.
The waterfall wasn't too far away now,
So the cheetah rushed off to find help.

The friends Leo had in the jungle
All raced to the bank right away.

They wanted so much to show Leo their thanks,
At last they had now found a way.

They climbed on the rocks through the rapids
And linked themselves up tail and paw.
An elephant wrapped his long trunk round a tree
And anchored them safe to the shore.

And when Leo got to the rapids
A lioness dipped down her head.
She lifted him gently out onto the bank,
"You're safe, Leo darling," she said.

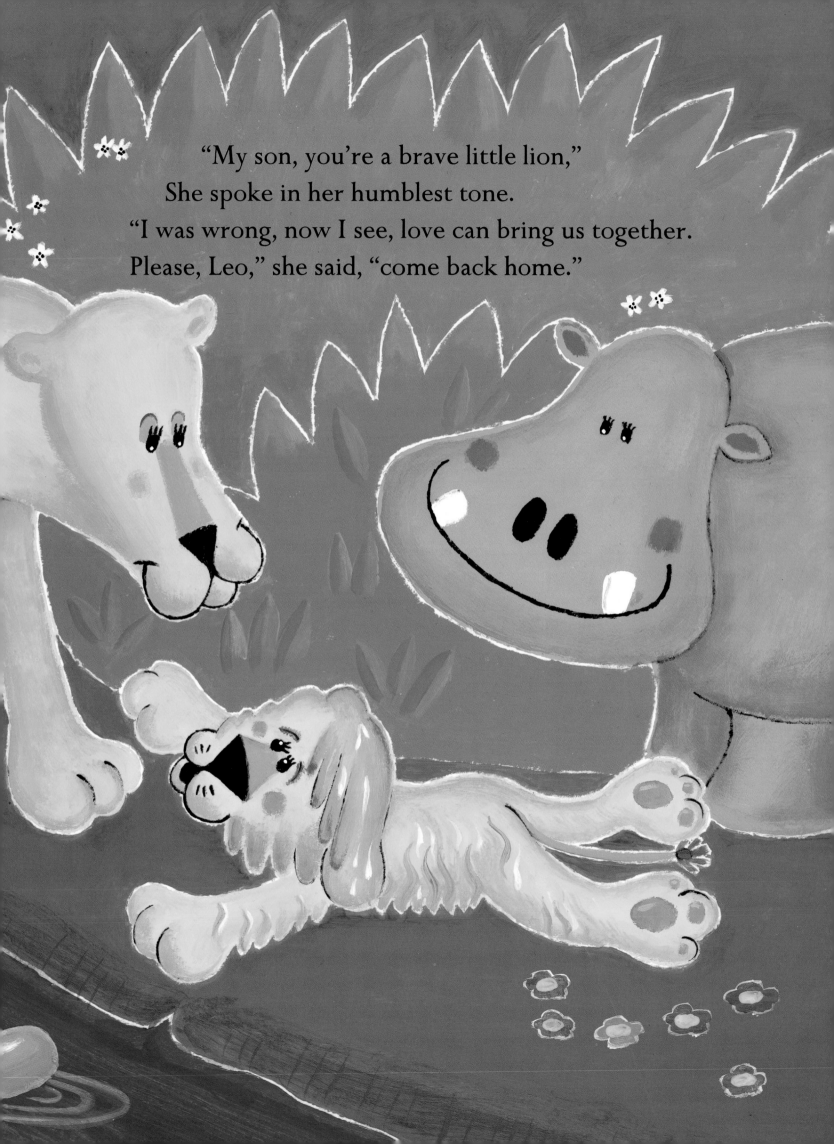

"My son, you're a brave little lion,"
She spoke in her humblest tone.
"I was wrong, now I see, love can bring us together.
Please, Leo," she said, "come back home."

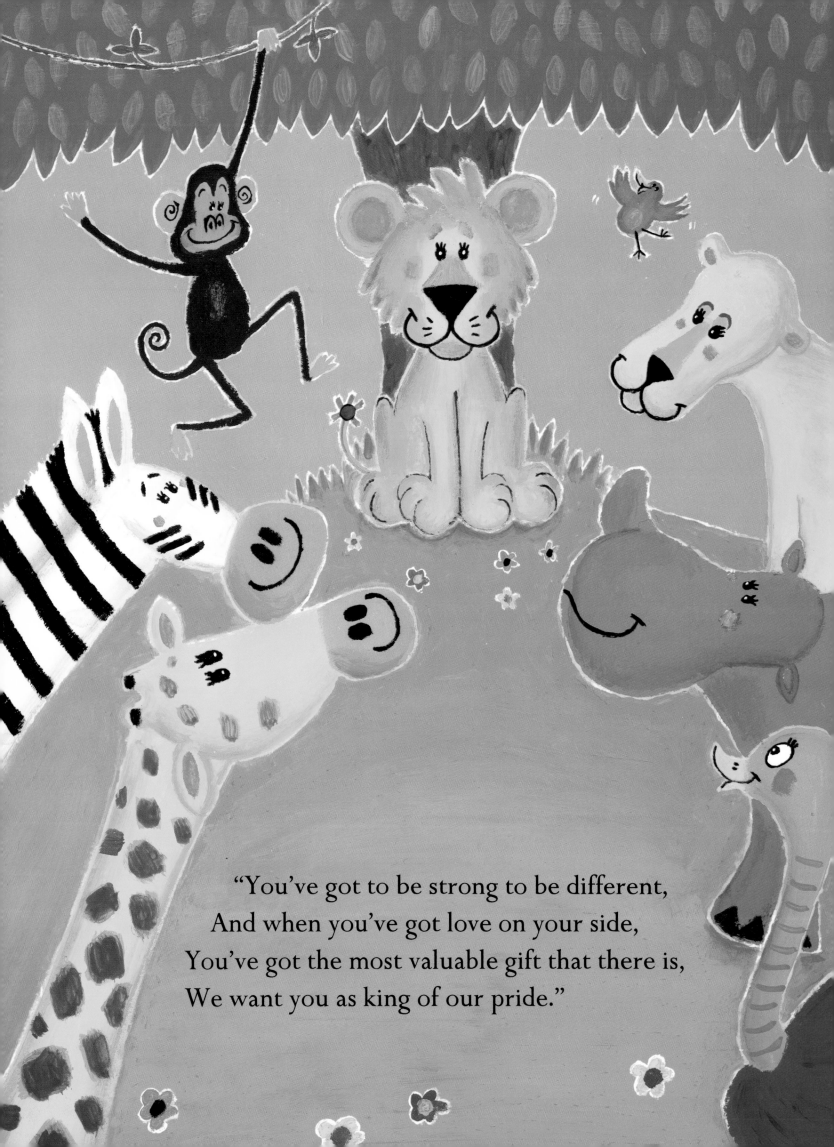

"You've got to be strong to be different,
And when you've got love on your side,
You've got the most valuable gift that there is,
We want you as king of our pride."